THIS WHERE'S WALDO? BOOK BELONGS TO:

HEY, WALDO FANS! FIVE INTREPID TRAVELERS ARE LOST IN EVERY SCENE! CAN YOU FIND THEM?

ODLAW   WIZARD WHITEBEARD   WENDA   WOOF   WALDO

AND IN EVERY SCENE, THE TRAVELERS HAVE EACH LOST SOMETHING PRECIOUS! CAN YOU FIND THESE ITEMS TOO?

WALDO'S KEY   WOOF'S BONE   WENDA'S CAMERA

WIZARD WHITEBEARD'S SCROLL   ODLAW'S BINOCULARS

FOR THE HONORARY
WALDO-WATCHERS—
MIKE, STEVE,
TERRY, AND EDDY

Copyright © 1987– 2017 by Martin Handford

All rights reserved. No part of this book
may be reproduced, transmitted, or stored
in an information retrieval system in any form
or by any means, graphic, electronic, or
mechanical, including photocopying, taping,
and recording, without prior written permission
from the publisher.

First U.S. paperback edition 2008

Library of Congress Cataloging-in-Publication
Data is available.

Library of Congress Catalog Card Number
2006046287

ISBN 978-0-7636-3043-0 (hardcover)
ISBN 978-0-7636-4215-0 (paperback)

19 20 21 WKT 24 23 22

Printed in Shenzhen, Guangdong, China

This book was typeset in Optima and Wallyfont.
The illustrations were done in ink and watercolor
or in ink and colored digitally.

Candlewick Press
99 Dover Street
Somerville, Massachusetts 02144

visit us at www.candlewick.com

THE GREAT PICTURE HUNT

HEY, WALDO FANS, WELCOME TO THE GREAT PICTURE HUNT. IT'S MORE THAN A BOOK— IT'S AN ART ADVENTURE! THE FUN STARTS ON THE NEXT PAGE, IN OLDAW'S PICTURE PANDEMONIUM, WHERE YOU'LL FIND 30 ENORMOUS PORTRAITS. EXAMINE THEM CAREFULLY, PICTURE PERUSERS, BECAUSE EACH ONE OF THE PORTRAIT SUBJECTS CAN BE FOUND SOMEWHERE ELSE IN THIS BOOK.

STARTING WITH THE VERY FIRST EXHIBIT, AND ENDING WITH EXHIBIT 11, YOUR CHALLENGE IS TO FIND THESE SLIPPERY SUBJECTS WHEREVER THEY MAY BE HIDING! AND OF COURSE, BESIDES OUR FRANTIC FRAME GAME, THERE ARE ALL THE USUAL SUBJECTS AND THEIR LOST OBJECTS TO SPOT IN EVERY SCENE.

BUT THE BUZZER DOESN'T SOUND THERE, BECAUSE THERE ARE ADDED TWISTS LIKE SPOT-THE-DIFFERENCES PUZZLES. AND AT THE BACK OF THE BOOK, YOU'LL FIND CHALLENGING CHECKLISTS OF MORE THINGS TO FIND!

NOW, GALLERY GAZERS, HAVE FUN, DON'T MAKE AN EXHIBITION OF YOURSELVES, AND LET THE GREAT PICTURE HUNT BEGIN!

Waldo

FIND:
WALDO—OUR YOUNG GALLERY GUIDE, WHO TRAVELS EVERYWHERE!
WOOF—WHO WAGS HIS NOT-SO-BRUSH- LIKE TAIL (WHICH IS ALL YOU CAN SEE!).
WENDA—WHO TAKES THE PICTURES (BUT DOESN'T PAINT THEM!).
WIZARD WHITEBEARD—THE OLD MASTER, WHO CASTS COLORFUL SPELLS!
ODLAW—WHO'S BEEN AN EXHIBIT IN MANY A ROGUE'S GALLERY!

AND DON'T FORGET MY LOST KEY, WOOF'S MISSING BONE, WENDA'S MISPLACED CAMERA, WIZARD WHITEBEARD'S MISLAID SCROLL, AND ODLAW'S ABSENT BINOCULARS.

EXHIBIT 1—ODLAW'S PICTURE PANDEMONIUM

WOW, WALDO FANS, WHAT PORTRAIT PANDEMONIUM! HAVE YOU EVER SEEN SO MANY YELLOW AND BLACK STRIPES IN ONE PLACE? STRIPE-TASTIC! WE'RE HERE IN ODLAW'S PICTURE GALLERY, AND JUST LOOK AT WHAT HIS ARTFUL ASSOCIATES HAVE CARRIED IN—30 PECULIAR PORTRAITS IN AN ODDITY OF FRAMES. AMAZING! THERE'S QUITE A CAST OF CHARACTERS IN THESE PAINTINGS, AND THEY ALL APPEAR AGAIN ELSEWHERE IN THE BOOK. AND PICTURE THIS: ONE OF THEM EVEN APPEARS SOMEWHERE IN THIS CRAZY CROWD! GOOD LUCK ON YOUR HUNT FOR THE PLACES WITH THE FACES. WHAT A PICTURE!

EXHIBIT 2—
A SPORTING LIFE
WELCOME, PICTURE HUNT PALS, TO MY
SPECIAL REPORT FROM THE LAND OF
SPORTS. FANTASTIC! IT'S LIKE THE OLYMPICS
EVERY DAY HERE, BUT WITH SO MANY
ATHLETIC EVENTS ON THE MENU, THERE'S NO
TIME LEFT FOR ANY REST AND RELAXATION.
BUT THERE'S NOTHING TOO STRENUOUS
ABOUT OUR MAIN EVENT, THE GREAT
PICTURE HUNT, SO KEEP YOUR EYES ON
THE BALL AND YOUR POINTER
FINGER READY. ON YOUR
MARK, GET SET, GO!

EXHIBIT 5—THE PINK PARADISE PARTY

IT'S SATURDAY NIGHT, THE TEMPERATURE IS RISING, AND IT LOOKS AS IF A RASH OF MUSICAL MAYHEM AND DISCO FEVER HAS BROKEN OUT IN THIS DIZZY DANCE HALL. WHEW! IT'S HOT! HIP HIP-HOPPERS, ROCK-AND-ROLLERS, AND BODY-AND-SOULERS—IT'S A PACKED-OUT, PARTYGOERS' PINK PARADISE. SO GET ON DOWN, CUT YOUR GROOVE, AND MAKE YOUR MOVES—IT'S TIME TO SHUFFLE YOUR FEET TO THE PICTURE HUNT BEAT!

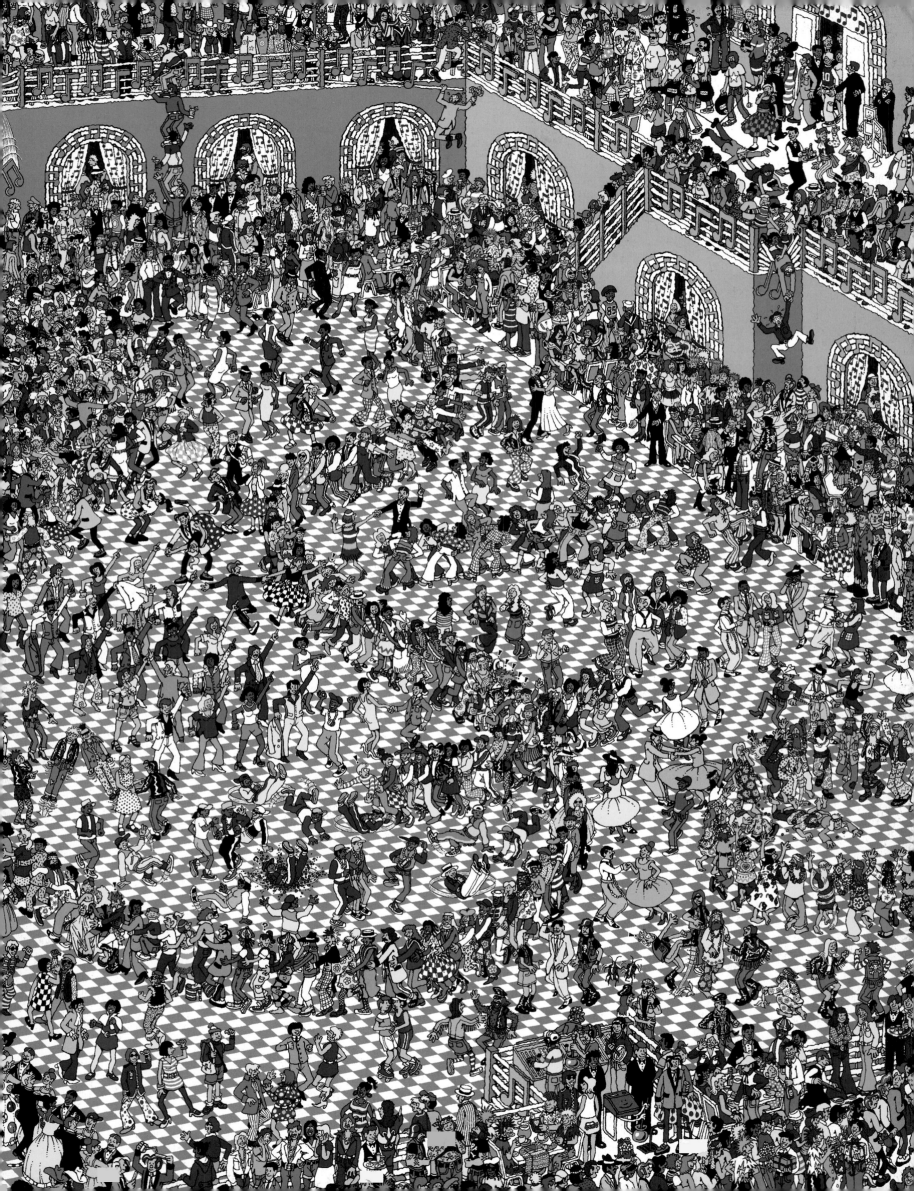

EXHIBIT 6—OLD FRIENDS

AH, PICTURE HUNT PALS, HOW I LOVE TO LOOK THROUGH MY SCRAPBOOKS OF MEMORIES AND SOUVENIRS. THIS PAGE IS ONE OF MY FAVORITES: A COLLAGE CRAMMED WITH FAMILIAR FACES FROM MY EARLIER ADVENTURES. FANTASTIC! EVEN THE MOST DEDICATED OF WALDO-WATCHERS AMONG YOU MAY HAVE TROUBLE RECOGNIZING ALL THE OLD FRIENDS HERE— IT'S QUITE A CHALLENGE. BUT HERE'S AN EASIER TEASER THAT ANYONE CAN DO: JUST LOOK AT THE CIRCLED FACES IN THE BORDER OF THIS FRAME, THEN SEE IF YOU CAN SPOT THEM IN THE SURROUNDING PICTURE.

EXHIBIT 7—OLD FRIENDS AGAIN

IT'S ALWAYS NICE WHEN FRIENDS CAN STAY A LITTLE LONGER. . . . HERE'S A COLLECTION OF PORTRAITS OF SOME OF THE OLD FRIENDS FROM NEXT DOOR—BUT IN SILHOUETTE FORM. CAN YOU MATCH UP THE BLAST-FROM-THE-PAST CHARACTERS ON THE PREVIOUS PAGE WITH THEIR SILHOUETTES HERE? JUST TO MAKE IT INTERESTING, SOME OF THEM ARE UPSIDE DOWN OR SIDEWAYS. SO, ONWARD AND UPWARD (AND DOWNWARD AND SIDEWAYS!), PICTURE HUNTERS!

EXHIBIT 8 — THE MONSTER MASTERPIECE

YIKES, SPIKES, AND SCALY SEGMENTS, I'M LOST IN THE LAND OF THE MONSTERS. WHAT A CREATURE FEATURE! WHO'S IN CHARGE HERE, ANYWAY? THE HELMETED HUNTERS OR THEIR QUARRELSOME QUARRY? YOU'D BETTER WATCH OUT FOR BOTH AS YOU DIVE INTO THIS MONSTER MAYHEM, ART FANS— THERE ARE STILL SOME PORTRAIT SUBJECTS TO FIND. WHAT A MONSTROSITY!

EXHIBIT 9—WALDOWORLD

WHAT A WEIRD AND WACKY WORLD WE'RE IN, GALLERY GAZERS—NOT JUST A WORLD OF WALDOS BUT A WORLD OF WHITEBEARDS, WENDAS, WOOFS, AND AN ODDITY OF ODLAWS AS WELL. AMAZING! BUT LOOK AGAIN. . . . THERE'S ONLY ONE REAL WALDO HERE, AND THE SAME GOES FOR MY FRIENDS, TOO. DON'T FORGET THAT YOU CAN TELL IF WE'RE THE GENUINE ARTICLES BY OUR CORRECT ARRANGEMENT OF STRIPES. SO CAST YOUR EYES ACROSS THIS COLLECTION OF IMPOSTERS AND IMPERSONATORS AND SEE IF YOU CAN FIND THE REAL US!

EXHIBIT 10—WALDOWORLD AGAIN

DON'T BE DAUNTED BY HAVING TO DALLY OVER THIS DIZZY DIORAMA OF DOPPELGANGERS, DEAR READERS. EVERYTHING IS NOT AS IT APPEARS. WE'RE ALL STILL HERE, BUT THIS TIME THERE ARE 20 VARIATIONS FROM THE SCENE ON THE LEFT. CAN YOU SPOT ALL THE DIFFERENCES? AND HAVE YOU FOUND THE REAL WHITEBEARD, WENDA, WOOF, AND ODLAW YET? IF YOU'RE STILL HAVING TROUBLE FINDING THE REAL US, WHY NOT CHECK OUT HOW WE LOOK IN THE KEY ON PAGE 3?

EXHIBIT 11—PIRATE PANORAMA

SHIVER ME TIMBERS, SHIPMATES, WHAT PERFIDIOUS PIRATE PANORAMA IS THIS? WOW! AMAZING! WE'VE SAILED THE SEVEN SEAS SEARCHING FOR THOSE 30 PESKY PORTRAIT PEOPLE, AND NOW THAT OUR JOURNEY IS ALMOST OVER, I JUST HOPE THE PIRATES DON'T MAKE THEM WALK THE PLANK! I'M SURE THEY WOULD RATHER BE MAROONED ON A DESERT ISLAND THAN MEET THESE BARMY BUCCANEERS. ALL HANDS ON DECK!

EXHIBIT 12—THE GREAT PORTRAIT EXHIBITION

OUR JOURNEY IS NOW OVER, WALDO FANS, BUT WHAT A FITTING FINALE—A FANTASTIC EXHIBITION IN A PROPER ART GALLERY! THE CROWD HERE SEEMS MORE WELCOMING THAN ODLAW'S ODD ENSEMBLE FROM THE FIRST SCENE. I'M ALSO REALLY PLEASED THAT ALL 30 OF THE CHARACTERS WE'VE BEEN SEARCHING FOR IN THE EARLIER SCENES APPEAR AGAIN HERE AMONG THE GALLERY GAZERS. SEE IF YOU CAN SPOT THEM AS THEY TRY TO BLEND INTO THE CROWD AND ENJOY THE SHOW. I HOPE YOU FOUND THEM IN THE PREVIOUS PAGES, TOO. IF NOT, THERE'S STILL PLENTY OF TIME TO DO SO—THE EXHIBITION NEVER CLOSES!

WHERE'S WALDO?

THE GREAT PICTURE HUNT!

CHECKLISTS & ANSWERS

Lots more things for Waldo-watchers to look for!

EXHIBIT 1—ODLAW'S PICTURE PANDEMONIUM

- A green-skinned pirate
- Two ghost imposters
- Five mummies
- A bandaged finger
- Two spiders
- A head and crossbones
- A drooping flower
- Two teddy tattoos
- A black cat
- The sun
- Eight striped witches' hats

- 14 ladders
- 12 vultures
- An upside-down skull and crossbones
- Four flying witches
- A pair of heart-shaped sunglasses
- Three spike-topped helmets
- A puzzled, fangless vampire
- A drinking straw
- A squashed Viking

EXHIBIT 2 — A SPORTING LIFE

- Hitting a hole in one
- A centaur circle
- A volleyball court
- Serving an ace
- A boxer saved by the belle
- Four under Pa
- The baseball batter's swing
- A pool table
- A Jim instructor
- Dancers at a soccer ball
- Team subs
- A marshal arts class
- Weight lifters pumping iron
- Shadowboxers
- A football quarterback
- Snow-peaked caps
- A pair of swimming trunks
- An archer with a long bow
- A steeplechase
- A pear skating

SPOT-THE-DIFFERENCES EXHIBIT 4— BROWN SAILORS & GREEN SCALERS AGAIN ANSWERS

- A missing tail-end
- An absent cloud
- A brown balloon
- A balloon number missing
- A missing tooth
- A missing lasso
- Some smoke missing
- A missing flag
- A monster without spots
- A backward number
- A flag number missing
- A missing monster
- An absent sailor
- A missing telescope
- A man with a yellow beard
- Some missing green slime
- An extra sailor
- A slime gun without a nozzle
- A brown sea creature
- A sailor in a white top

EXHIBIT 5—THE PINK PARADISE PARTY

- Two skates on skates
- A broken heel
- A heavy-metal guitarist
- Two banana skins
- A pencil skirt
- Ball room dancers
- Two bugs jitterbugging
- A sole singer
- Dancers tripping on beads
- A Miniskirt

- A tea-shirt
- Two foxtrotters
- Platform shoes
- Some disc jockeys
- Oliver Twisting
- A Duke box and jukebox
- Dancing the knight away
- Beehive hairdos
- Squares square-dancing
- Two doormen

EXHIBIT 6—OLD FRIENDS

- A lady in a blue ball gown
- A snowman
- A monster in a man-suit
- A red astronaut
- A woman with a green bag
- A pirate surfing
- A thirsty boy
- A cook with a dough nut
- A crab clipping a toenail
- A hippo with a jumbo-size toothbrush
- A pole vaulter taking a break
- A rude statue
- A bullfrog
- A man holding a flower
- A man in a manhole
- A horse-drawn wagon
- A woman with a clipboard
- A swimmer in shades
- A dog in the shade
- A woman holding a hairbrush

EXHIBIT 8—THE MONSTER MASTERPIECE

- Salt and pepper shakers
- A ropey snakebite
- A monster wearing a napkin
- A tail lassoing a foot
- Two hunters using hankies
- A raft made from snakes
- A ticklish monster
- A snake tripping up hunters
- A pointed helmet prodding a hunter
- A monster munching timber
- One round shield
- Six arrows rebounding off monsters
- A swimming race
- A bunch of flowers
- A log stuck on a horn
- A monster wielding three swords
- A hunter held upside down
- A long tongue lassoing a leg
- A monster chewing spears
- Two hunter-boys sliding

EXHIBIT 11—PIRATE PANORAMA

- Seven bottles
- Diving boards
- A massage in a bottle
- A giant wave
- A school of whales
- A pirate riding the serf
- Five birds
- A deck of cards
- Seven flags
- A pirate walking the plank
- A dessert island
- 11 cannons
- The deep blue C
- Eight fins
- A pirate with an ax and a cutlass
- A tap
- Lobster beds
- Four cannonballs
- A two-foot gun barrel
- Two colored patches

SPOT-THE-DIFFERENCES EXHIBIT 10— WALDOWORLD AGAIN ANSWERS

- A Wenda wearing a red skirt
- A Whitebeard wearing a red hat
- A Waldo whose stripes have shifted
- A Whitebeard whose staff is missing
- A hat that has lost its pompom
- A Waldo in striped pants
- A Wenda who has lost her glasses
- A Woof with a longer tail
- A missing walking stick
- A spotted Odlaw
- A wizard beard that has changed color
- A Wenda with vertical stripes
- An Odlaw in yellow
- A walking stick missing a tip
- An Odlaw wearing blue-and-white tights
- An Odlaw wearing different glasses
- An Odlaw missing a hat
- A Woof missing a tail
- A Waldo no longer smiling
- A missing wizard

EXHIBIT 12—THE GREAT PORTRAIT EXHIBITION

- 19 flowers
- A woman guitarist
- A leaking watercolor
- Two dueling artists
- 11 horses
- Four brooms
- An empty red frame
- Two cavewomen
- A very long white beard
- Nine fish
- An artist with seven brushes
- A gray donkey
- A rude shield
- Two brushes in a hatband
- A hungry wolf
- A red bow tie
- An artist with a big brush
- Five stools
- Red-and-yellow striped sleeves
- A cracked vase

AND JUST ONE MORE THING . . .

Why not brush up on your math with this arithmetic problem? Add the number of frames containing pictures of men in Exhibit 1 to the number of blue picture frames in Exhibit 7. Then subtract the number of triangular frames in Exhibit 12.